The Artist and Me

To Jackson Peacock, who first told me stories—S.P.

To my sons, who make me a better person—S.C.

The Artist and Me

WRITTEN BY Shane Peacock
ILLUSTRATED BY Sophie Casson

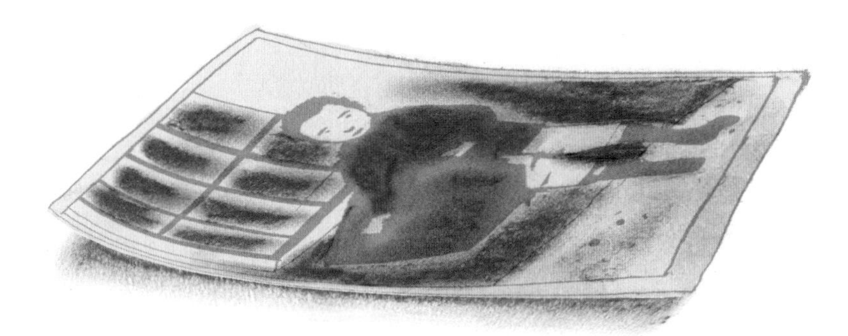

Owlkids Books

In the beautiful countryside in southern France near the town of Arles long ago, I used to do an ugly thing.

I tormented someone. I was mean to him.

But he wasn't just anyone.

He was a crazy man. He had wild red hair and a short red beard and a dream. His dream, he told anyone who would listen, was to tell the truth by painting pictures.

That made me laugh, and I did it loudly. I made sure others heard me.

Everyone I knew made fun of him.

EXPOSITION
VAN GOGH
MUSÉE DE
AVRIL-

There were many reasons to laugh.

He painted awful pictures.

They had bright hues that didn't match—colors weren't supposed to go like that.

They pictured people who didn't look the way they ought to look—and funny flowers and shining streets and strange starry skies. It wasn't right.

But sometimes his art made me wonder. And if I saw him sitting alone at a café in Arles, staring off into the distance, I would walk nearby, because he sometimes propped his paintings against his table.

I would make sure
that no one was watching
and then steal long looks
at what he had done.

But I kept being mean to him. In crowds, of course, since that is what cowards do. "There goes the fool," adults would say.

"A useless fool!" I'd laugh with them.

There was proof that we were right. No one ever bought his art. He was very poor. That was not to be admired.

We called him horrible names. We threw things at him. It made us almost giddy.

At times he scowled at us. Other times he didn't care.

He kept painting. He painted every day, all the time, no matter the weather or how he was feeling or what we did or said to him.

"I must tell the truth," he would keep repeating. He was on a mission. I wondered what my mission was.

"But he is crazy," I reminded myself.

Then, one day, I saw him near a roadway far out in the countryside. I was alone, chasing something—a rabbit, perhaps—and came upon him suddenly.

He was sitting before his easel with his back to me, staring out over a wheat field, and crows were approaching. It seemed he hadn't seen or heard me, though I was very close to him. I should have heard him breathing. But he made no sound at all.

I knew that if I moved, made so much as a tiny noise, he would turn and see me—me, who had been so mean to him.

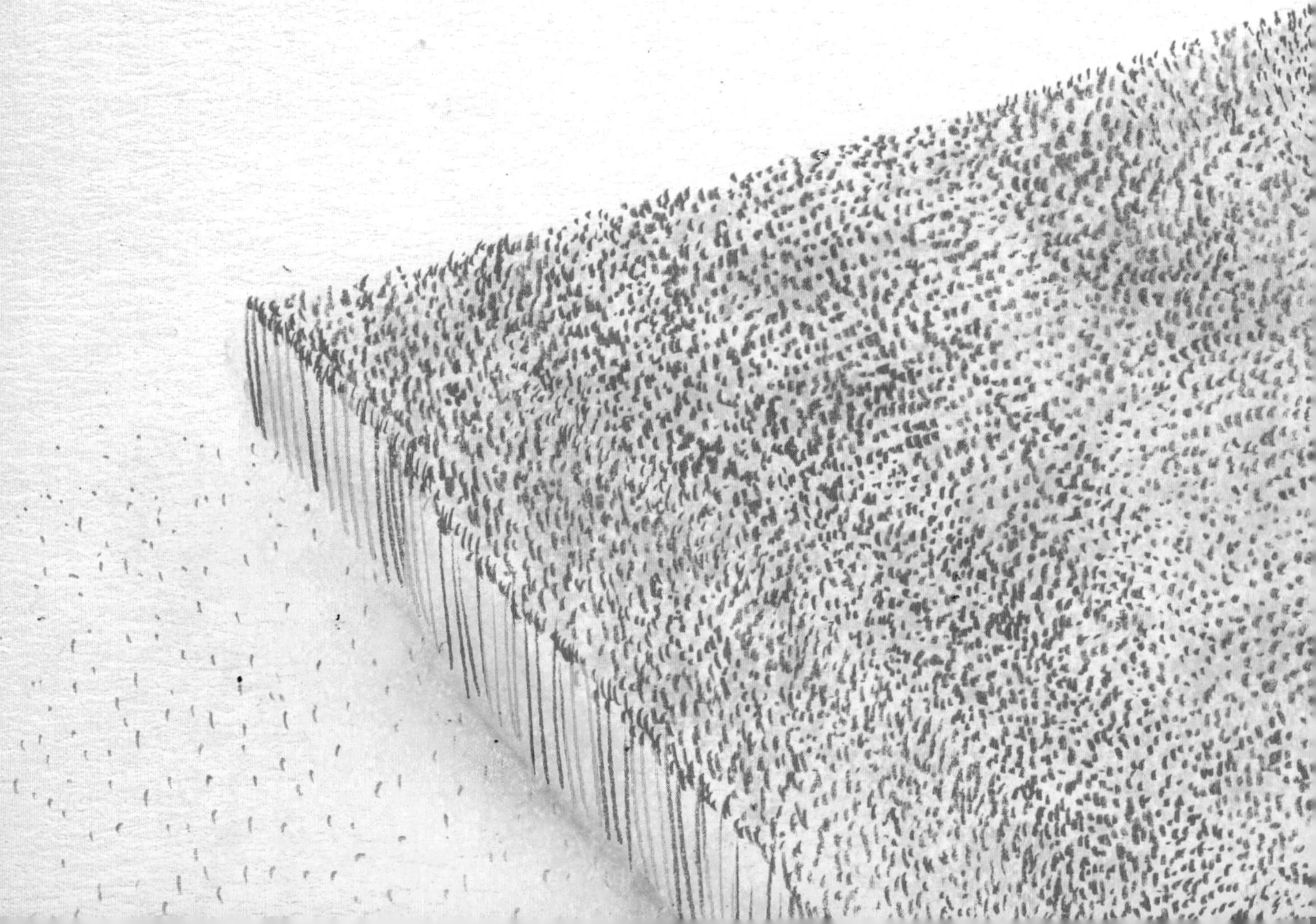

I was terrified. My knees went weak. My eyes widened. I almost fell over. And for an instant the world was bigger and brighter than it had ever been.

I stared out at the landscape before him. The sky was blue but boiling with violet. The wheat field was brown but shimmered like gold. Everything swayed and didn't seem exactly as it should. Or maybe it did.

Somehow, he sensed I was there. He turned and looked at me. His face was glowing. It was like the pictures I had seen of saints in churches.

He knew I was frightened. He smiled. He stood up and walked toward me.

I shrank back. He reached out.

And he offered me his painting.

"Go on," he said kindly. "Take it."

I refused, of course. I plucked up my courage and ran.

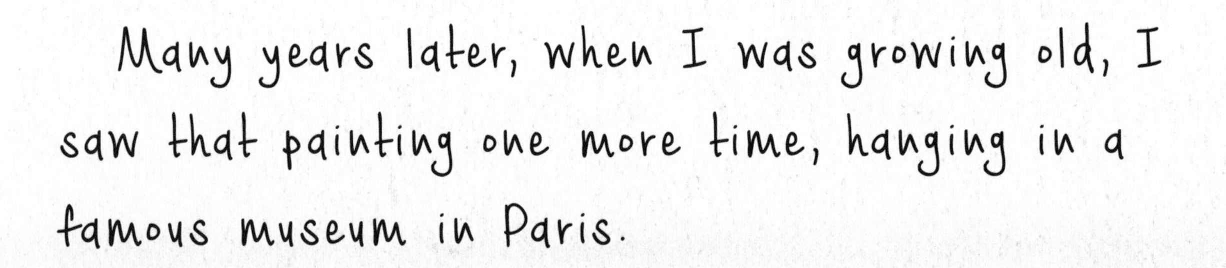

Many years later, when I was growing old, I saw that painting one more time, hanging in a famous museum in Paris.

It is one of his many masterpieces.

A treasure no money can buy.

I don't laugh at
him anymore.

Vincent

The Dutch artist Vincent van Gogh was nearing his 35th birthday when he came to Arles in southern France in 1888, but he already seemed like an old man. A difficult and emotional person, he'd always had a hard time fitting in, whether as the son of a minister in a large family, a troubled student, or an apprentice in the art-dealing business. Eventually, he decided to become an artist, a deep commitment that was more like a religious calling than a job to him. Yet he remained an outsider, sensitive and brilliant, with his own way of seeing and painting the world.

Riveted on his mission, dressed in dirty clothes, he walked the streets and countryside of Europe carrying his heavy painter's easel, working long hours, staring at subjects and attacking canvases with gobs of paint and rainbows of color. He was often publicly bullied and called a fool. Children were among his enemies, laughing at his bizarre art and throwing things at him; the ridicule increased after his mind became unhinged and he entered an insane asylum.

In the summer of 1890, Vincent died in mysterious circumstances in a village near Paris. He'd sold just one picture during his life and his work had received little notice. Today, some of his paintings are worth more than 100 million dollars and others are absolutely priceless. To many, he is now the greatest artist who ever lived.

Author's Note

I have always wanted to write about Vincent van Gogh. He is, to me, a hero. He didn't just want to be an artist, he believed in art. He lived as an outcast and in poverty but never gave up on his dream, and he didn't care if his paintings were well received or not. He stands today as a symbol of someone who lived a life that wasn't about making money or being famous but about doing what he believed in, no matter what. That is a great lesson for all of us, and certainly for me. Like all writers, I often struggle to trust myself to create my own sorts of stories, instead of the ones that others might want me to write or that are popular, and to stay at my work despite its challenges.

Vincent's passions and his unusual ways created all sorts of enemies. The bully in this story is a child, based on the many children who teased Vincent during his life. This boy taunts the painter because he is different and because others are doing the same. The boy goes along with the crowd and with his childish instincts. But deep down, he senses the truth – this hard-working "crazy" man is creating magical paintings that allow people to see the world in a brand-new way. And later, when the boy is an old man, and he visits the great gallery with his grandson, he realizes how terribly wrong he was, not just about Vincent's art, but about being a bully of any sort. Bullying was hurtful and a waste of his time, when he could have been on a "mission," too.

Sources

Callow, Philip. *Vincent Van Gogh: A Life.* Washington, DC: Rowman & Littlefield, 1996.

Naifeh, Steven, and Gregory White Smith. *Van Gogh: The Life.* New York: Random House, 2011.

Stone, Irving, ed. *Dear Theo: The Autobiography of Vincent Van Gogh.* New York: Plume, 1995.

Acknowledgments

First thanks should go to someone named Vincent van Gogh, whose inspiring life and work, in turn, inspired this story. The best biography of this great man, a monumental work in itself, *Van Gogh: The Life* by Steven Naifeh and Gregory White Smith, was hugely important in my research. It is almost all one needs when investigating the artist's life.

Karen Li and I met almost by accident but were immediately on the same page, it seemed, and remained that way throughout the creation of *The Artist and Me*. Her interest in this "odd" story, her belief in it and in my ability to tell it, never wavered. It is wonderful to work with an editor in whom you have such confidence and trust.

And of course this endeavor would amount to nothing without Sophie Casson and her beautiful art. She rose to the task of bringing my story to life and being the artist who illuminated THE artist with great insight and imagination.

And finally, thanks to my family, Sophie, Hadley, Sam, and Johanna, who live with a struggling artist every day of their lives. —S.P.

Owlkids Books acknowledges the financial support of the Canada Council for the Arts, the Ontario Arts Council, the Government of Canada through the Canada Book Fund (CBF) and the Government of Ontario through the Ontario Media Development Corporation's Book Initiative for our publishing activities.

Published in Canada by
Owlkids Books Inc.
10 Lower Spadina Avenue
Toronto, ON M5V 2Z2

Published in the United States by
Owlkids Books Inc.
1700 Fourth Street
Berkeley, CA 94710

Library and Archives Canada Cataloguing in Publication

Peacock, Shane, author
The artist and me / written by Shane Peacock ; illustrated by Sophie Casson.

ISBN 978-1-77147-138-1 (bound)

1. Gogh, Vincent van, 1853-1890--Juvenile fiction. I. Casson, Sophie, illustrator II. Title.

PS8581.E234A78 2016 jC813'.54 C2015-906009-5

Library of Congress Control Number: 2015948497

Edited by: Karen Li
Designed by: Alisa Baldwin

Manufactured in Dongguan, China, in August 2016, by Toppan Leefung Packaging & Printing (Dongguan) Co., Ltd.
Job #BAYDC21/R1

B C D E F

Publisher of Chirp, chickaDEE and OWL
www.owlkidsbooks.com

Owlkids Books is a division of